E
WAT

Watson, Mary

The butterfly seeds

$16.00

| DATE | | | |
|---|---|---|---|
| JUN 1 7 1996 | | | |
| AUG 2 9 1996 | | | |
| JUL 3 1 1999 | | | |
| AUG X 3 2000 | | | |
| MAY 1 4 2002 | | | |
| JUL 1 0 2003 | | | |
| AUG 0 8 2007 | | | |
| | | | |
| | | | |
| | | | |

BAKER & TAYLOR

*Mary Watson*

# The BUTTERFLY SEEDS

TAMBOURINE BOOKS  NEW YORK

Library of Congress Cataloging in Publication Data
Watson, Mary, 1953–
The butterfly seeds / by Mary Watson. — 1st ed.   p.  cm.
Summary: When his family comes to America,
Jake brings special seeds that produce
a wonderful reminder of his grandfather.
[1. Emigration and immigration—Fiction.
2. Grandfathers—Fiction.]   I. Title.
PZ7.W3278Bu 1995 [E]—dc20 95-13250 CIP AC
ISBN 0-688-14132-3 (tr). — ISBN 0-688-14133-1 (le)

1  3  5  7  9  10  8  6  4  2
First edition

*In memory of my grandfather,*
*and the many happy hours I spent with him*
*in his greenhouse.*

Jake's house was empty, except for the overstuffed trunk in the middle of the floor.

"Sit on it, Mama," Papa instructed.

His sisters giggled as they watched Mama bounce up and down while Papa tried to close the latch.

But Jake just stared out the window. He kept thinking about how much he would miss Grandpa.

When Grandpa came to say good-bye,
he brought presents for everyone. But he
gave Jake something special.

"They're butterfly seeds," Grandpa said,
poking around in the little tin box. "Just
plant them in your new garden, and, like
magic, you'll have hundreds of butterflies."

"Are you sure they will grow in America,
Grandpa?" Jake asked sadly. Grandpa
pressed the little box tightly into Jake's
hand and nodded.

That evening, Jake's family crowded onto the deck of the great S.S. *Celtic.* Many of the passengers were carrying balls of yarn with the ends trailing over the side of the boat.

When the ship pulled away from the dock, those left behind held the ends and watched the lines stretch out across the ocean. Jake could barely see Grandpa when his yarn-line was pulled from his hand. He reached into his pocket to make sure Grandpa's seeds were safe.

That night, the ship tossed, rolling the
passengers back and forth in their narrow
bunk beds. Jake couldn't sleep. He reached
over and slipped his hand into his jacket
pocket.

"What do you have there?" Benny asked.
The boys moved closer to the dim cabin
light.

"They're butterfly seeds," Jake said,
opening the tin.

"What kind of seeds?" a few sleepy-eyed
children asked as they crawled down from
their bunk.

Then Jake told them about Grandpa's
seeds, and the beautiful butterfly garden
he would plant in America.

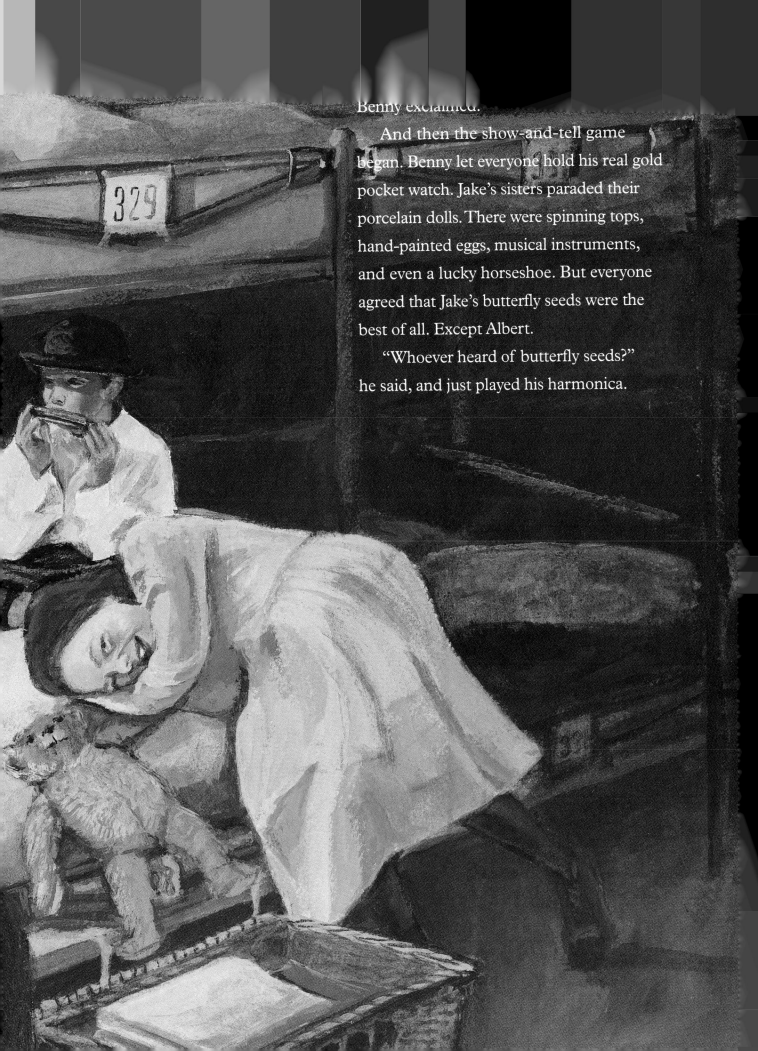

Benny exclaimed.

And then the show-and-tell game began. Benny let everyone hold his real gold pocket watch. Jake's sisters paraded their porcelain dolls. There were spinning tops, hand-painted eggs, musical instruments, and even a lucky horseshoe. But everyone agreed that Jake's butterfly seeds were the best of all. Except Albert.

"Whoever heard of butterfly seeds?" he said, and just played his harmonica.

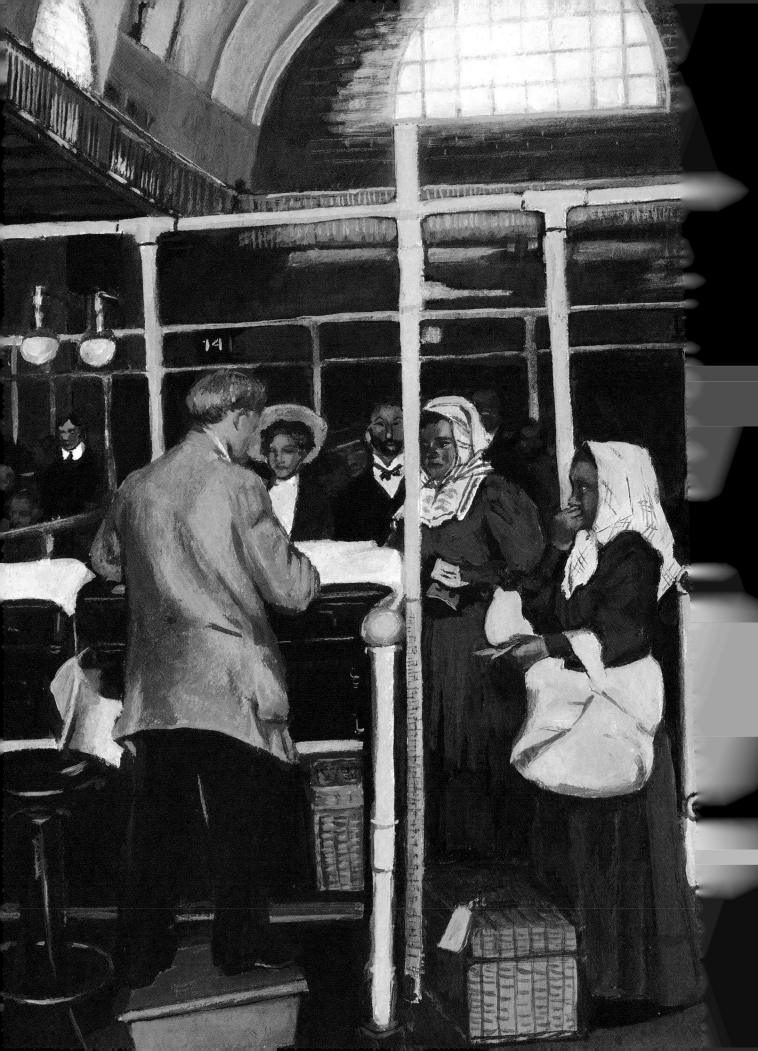

After two long weeks, the ship docked in New York. Papa held tightly to Mama and the children as everyone was herded onto the waiting ferryboats.

When the ferries reached Ellis Island, the passengers were shuffled into long lines to be inspected. Jake's heart raced, as he slowly inched up in line. He wondered if they would take away his seeds. The inspectors looked in Jake's ears and eyes—but not in his pockets. Grandpa's seeds were safe!

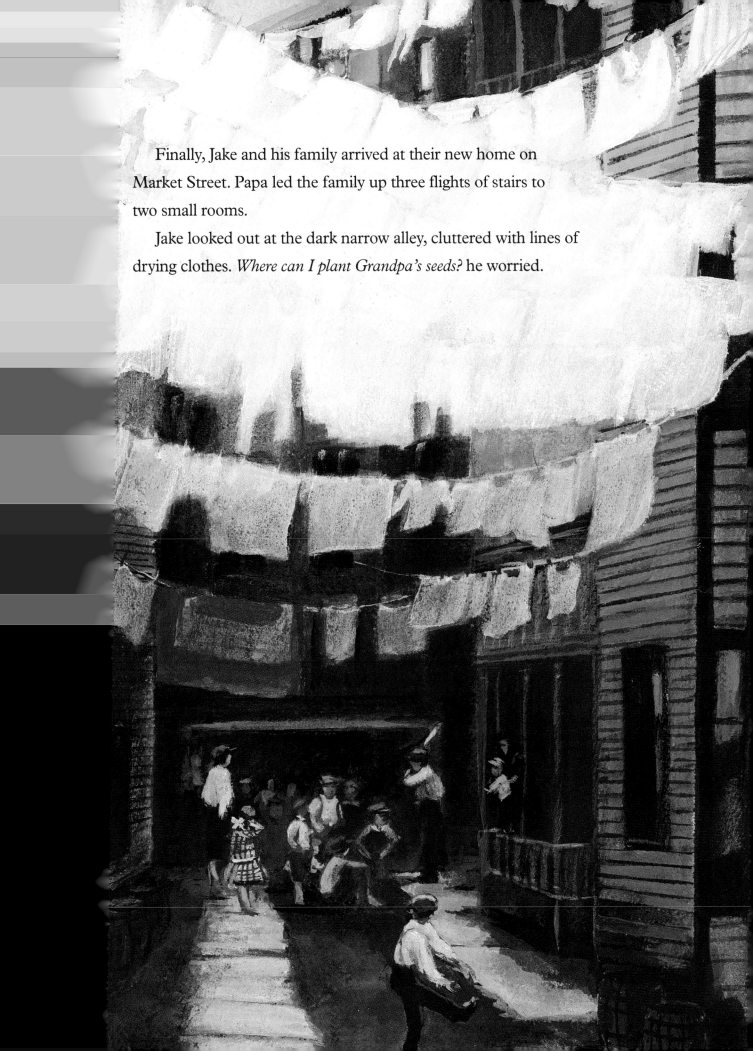

Finally, Jake and his family arrived at their new home on Market Street. Papa led the family up three flights of stairs to two small rooms.

Jake looked out at the dark narrow alley, cluttered with lines of drying clothes. *Where can I plant Grandpa's seeds?* he worried.

The next morning, Jake was up early. Below, he spotted a fruit vendor emptying a crate of apples into his cart.

"Could I have that empty crate, sir?" he yelled down.

Before Mr. Gargiulo could figure out where the question had come from, Jake was standing breathlessly beside him.

"I'm going to make a window box . . . so I can plant my grandpa's seeds in it . . . and that's why I need the crate," he blurted out.

"You can have the crate, boy, but I don't think it's any good for planting seeds." Mr. Gargiulo wiggled his fingers between the slats.

"All you need is a piece of burlap to fix that," called Mr. Lingchow, the fish peddler.

He emptied his catch into an icy bin and handed Jake the empty bag. Jake opened the seam with his pocketknife and spread the burlap evenly inside the crate.

Jake hurried across the street to
the blacksmith shop to show Papa. It
was Papa's first day at his new job, and
he didn't pay much attention when Jake
asked for his advice.

"I need a way to keep this crate from
falling off our windowsill," Jake shouted over
the ring of the anvil.

"Maybe I can help you," someone
hollered. It was Mr. O'Malley, the shop
owner. He knew just what Jake needed. He
hammered two bars of red-hot metal into a
strong pair of window-box hangers.

After work, Papa nailed the box into place. Jake rigged up a clothesline and a pulley to hoist up buckets of dirt from the alley. All of the neighborhood children wanted to help. All except for Albert, who played his harmonica instead.

It was a hot summer. Jake and his new friends climbed the fire escape every day to check the window box. They would hang over the railing and search through the bushy plants for butterflies.

"Maybe your silly old grandpa got the seeds mixed up," Albert would mutter.

Jake began to wonder if Grandpa's seeds were magic or just a story made up for a homesick boy.

Then one day the sky rumbled, and a sudden shower drenched the hot, steaming streets.

When the sun reappeared, merchants and shoppers filled the street once more. The children went back to their play.

Suddenly, Mr. Gargiulo called out, "Look at that beautiful butterfly."

The children chased the butterfly through the crowded street until it flew up to Jake's window box.

"Look at them all!" Albert shouted.

Jake heard Albert's yell and opened his window.

"They're finally here, Grandpa!" Jake whispered, as if Grandpa were listening. "Your butterflies are here . . . and they like America too."